30518

DISCARD

Hamburg Township Library

LIFE IN STRANGE PLACES

Extraterrestrial Life
life beyond Earth?

Harry Breidahl

This edition first published in 2002 in the United States of America by Chelsea House Publishers, a subsidiary of Haights Cross Communications.

All rights reserved. No part of this publication may be reproduced or transmitted in any form or by any means without the written permission of the publisher.

Chelsea House Publishers
1974 Sproul Road, Suite 400
Broomall, PA 19008-0914

The Chelsea House world wide web address is www.chelseahouse.com

Library of Congress Cataloging-in-Publication Data Applied for.
ISBN 0-7910-6616-9

First published in 2001 by
Macmillan Education Australia Pty Ltd
627 Chapel Street, South Yarra, Australia, 3141

Copyright © Harry Breidahl 2001

Edited by Angelique Campbell-Muir
Text design by Cristina Neri
Cover design by Cristina Neri
Printed in China

Acknowledgements
The author and the publishers are grateful to the following for permission to reproduce copyright material:

Cover photographs: Star background, courtesy PhotoDisc; *Stardust* approaching Comet Wild 2, courtesy Photolibrary.com/NASA/SPL; Utopia Planitia (on Mars) from *Viking 2*, courtesy Auscape/NASA/Tom Stack.

AAP/Associated Press, p. 15 (bottom); AAP/Associated Press AP-DIG, p. 14; AAP/David J. Phillip, p. 15 (top); Astrovisuals/NASA, pp. 4–5, 13, 18, 21 (both), 22, 29; Astrovisuals/NASA/JPL Photo, p. 27 (top); Auscape/NASA/JPL/Tsado — Tom Stack, p. 27 (bottom); Auscape/NASA/Tom Stack, pp. 1, 3 (middle), 5 (bottom right), 13 (top), 28–29; Auscape/Tsado/NASA — Tom Stack, pp. 5 (top left), 17 (bottom); Austral/SS/Universal, pp. 3 (top), 6; Australian Picture Library/Corbis, pp. 11 (top), 26; Dr. D.W. Larson/University of Guelph, p. 9 (top); Mary Evans Picture Library, p. 11 (bottom); NASA/JPL/Caltech, pp. 24, 25; National Oceanic and Atmospheric Administration/Department of Commerce/OAR/National Undersea Research Program (NURP), p. 9 (bottom); PhotoDisc, pp. 4 (bottom left), 7 (bottom), 20; Photolibrary.com/A.B. Dowsett/SPL, 7 (top); Photolibrary.com/NASA/Science Photo Library, pp. 5 (top right), 17 (top), 19, 23; Photolibrary.com/Science Photo Library, p. 10; Photolibrary.com/Tim Everett, pp. 4 (middle right), 8.

While every care has been taken to trace and acknowledge copyright the publishers tender their apologies for any accidental infringement where copyright has proved untraceable. Where the attempt has been unsuccessful, the publishers welcome information that would redress the situation.

Contents

Is there life beyond the Earth?	4
Background	
Searching for extraterrestrials	6
Studying life on Earth for clues	8
Looking for life on Mars	
Mars through telescopes	10
Sampling Martian soil for microbes	12
Fossilized Martian microbes	14
Looking for life elsewhere in the Solar System	
Extraterrestrial life on Europa	16
The origin of life on Titan	18
Signs of early life on asteroids and comets	20
Space technology	
On the way to Titan and a comet	22
Continuing the search for extraterrestrial life	24
Profile of an astronomer and exobiologist	
Dr. Carl Sagan	26
Exploring new frontiers	
Looking beyond the Solar System	28
Finding out more	30
Glossary	31
Index	32

SEARCHING THE WORLD WIDE WEB

If you have access to the world wide web, you have a gateway to some fascinating information. You can also use the web to see photographs, watch short videos and even search for particular topics. In this book, useful search words appear like this— astrobiology. Useful books and web sites are also listed on page 30.

Is there life beyond the Earth?

Humans have been thinking and dreaming about extraterrestrial life (life beyond the Earth) for ages. However, the serious study of extraterrestrial life is quite new. It is called astrobiology, or exobiology.

Astrobiology involves looking for:
- life on the planets, moons, asteroids and comets of our Solar System
- other solar systems beyond our own
- life in Earth's extreme environments (and how that life began).

HOW DO YOU SAY IT?

Europa: you-**row**-pah
extraterrestrial: ek-**stra**-ter-**rest**-re-al
exobiology: **eks**-o-by-ol-ogy

Life on Earth is far more widespread than once thought. The discovery of life in extreme environments gives us clues to what life beyond the Earth may be like (see pages 8–9).

Icy comets are the leftover pieces from when the Solar System was formed. Comets may be able to teach us about the start of life on Earth (see pages 20–21).

🚀 **Europa** is one of four large moons that belong to the planet Jupiter. Europa has a smooth icy surface which, scientists think, may hide an ocean. If this ocean does exist, could it contain life? (See pages 16–17.)

The second largest moon in the Solar System is Saturn's moon 🚀 **Titan**. Titan is incredibly cold, but its hazy atmosphere may be a lot like Earth's early atmosphere (see pages 18–19).

Of all the planets in our 🚀 **Solar System**, 🚀 **Mars** is the most like Earth. It has surface features like old river valleys and dry lake beds. This suggests that there may have been life on Mars in the past (see pages 10–15).

Astronomers (people who study objects in space) have found planets orbiting other stars. Now we know there is more than one solar system, the chances of life beyond Earth may be even greater (see pages 28–29).

Background
searching for extraterrestrials

The most difficult thing about searching for extraterrestrial life is the fact that space is incredibly big. In our Solar System, Earth's nearest planetary neighbour is Venus. Venus is 41 million kilometers (25 million miles) away from Earth. Pluto, the planet furthest from Earth, is a staggering 5.75 billion kilometers (3.5 billion miles) away. Beyond our Solar System, there are countless other stars in the Universe. The distances between stars are vast and are measured in light years. (One light year equals around 10 trillion kilometers.)

By using telescopes and **robot spacecraft**, astronomers now know enough about the Solar System to narrow the search for extraterrestrials down to a few of the more likely targets. These include:

- Mars, which may once have been home to some simple forms of life
- Europa, which may have some form of life in an ocean below its icy surface
- Titan, which is incredibly cold but may hold clues to the origin of life
- Comets and asteroids, which may also hold clues to the origin of life.

In science fiction stories, extraterrestrials are usually human-like beings. Some are friendly but many are shown as villains.

Astrobiologists now believe they will not find large organisms (living things) of any kind anywhere in our Solar System. However, they are still looking for extraterrestrials. They expect these extraterrestrials to be incredibly small, similar to microbes (microscopic organisms) found on Earth.

Astrobiologists believe that only Earth-like planets can support human-like organisms. As there are no other planets like Earth in our Solar System, they are now looking further into the Universe for Earth-like planets. Perhaps one of these planets is inhabited by organisms that are looking back at us!

Studying life on Earth for clues

Earth is the only place where we know life exists. The good news is that we know a great deal about life on Earth. This means that the search for extraterrestrial life is being helped by the study of life on Earth. Astrobiologists now know that life can survive in extreme environments such as in hot springs, inside rocks in Antarctica's dry valleys, and around **hydrothermal vents**.

By studying the life found in these sorts of extreme environments, astrobiologists are learning more about life that may be found beyond the Earth. They are finding out what kind of life to look for, and what sorts of places to look for it. They have learned that they should be looking for microbes (such as **bacteria**) rather than large organisms (such as plants and animals). Although there are no other places in the Solar System where humans could survive, there are places that are similar to Earth's extreme environments where microbes may survive.

HOW DO YOU SAY IT?
hydrothermal: **hi**-drow-**thur**-mal

The vivid colors in the water around this hot spring are made by microbes that thrive in extremely hot water. If microbes can live in such extreme environments on Earth, could they be found in similar places on Mars?

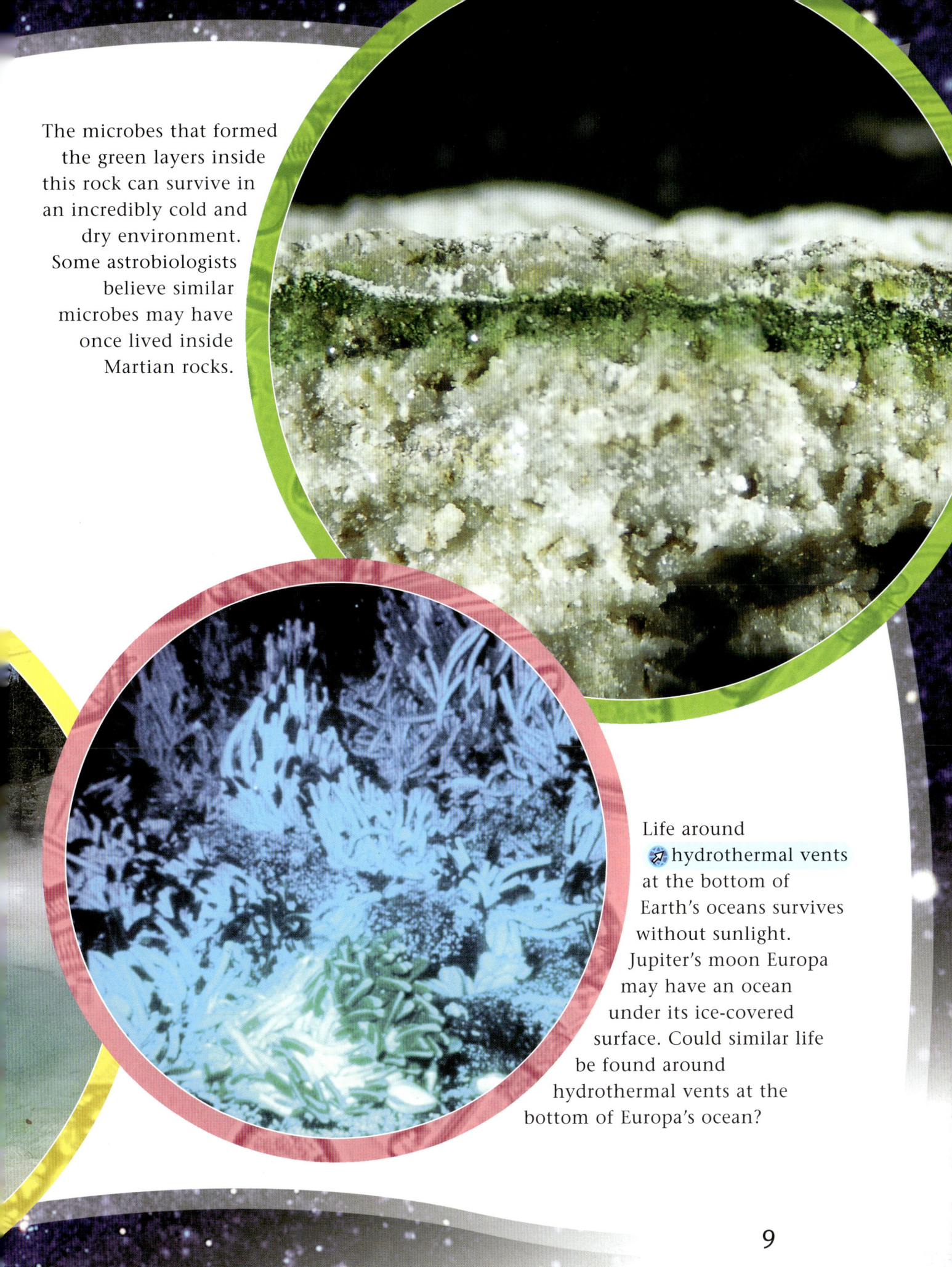

The microbes that formed the green layers inside this rock can survive in an incredibly cold and dry environment. Some astrobiologists believe similar microbes may have once lived inside Martian rocks.

Life around 🧭 hydrothermal vents at the bottom of Earth's oceans survives without sunlight. Jupiter's moon Europa may have an ocean under its ice-covered surface. Could similar life be found around hydrothermal vents at the bottom of Europa's ocean?

Looking for life on Mars

Mars through telescopes

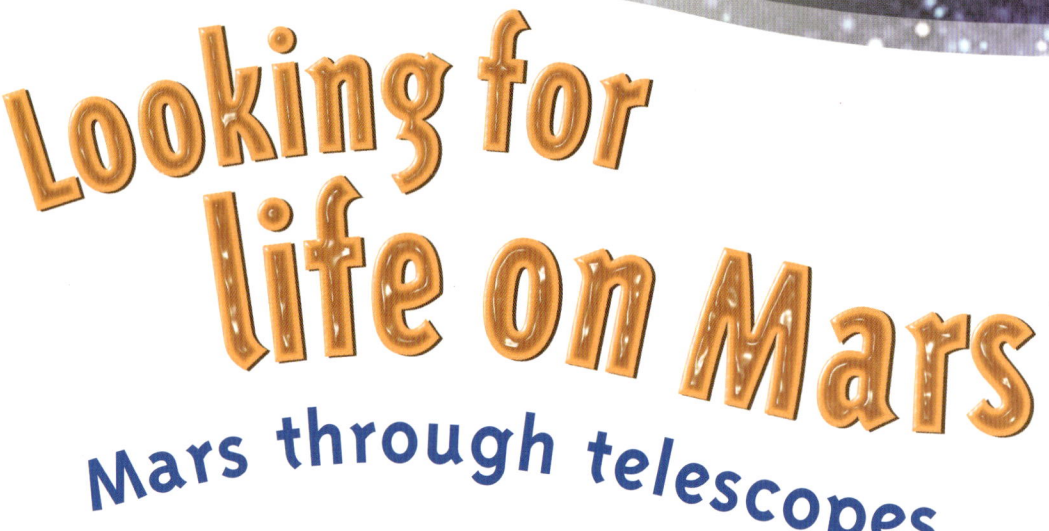

Mars is the Earth's second closest planetary neighbor. It looks like a reddish star as it wanders across the night sky. However, it was not until the invention of the telescope that we could actually see the surface of Mars. In 1877, an Italian astronomer called 📍 Giovanni Schiaparelli used a telescope to see what he thought was a network of strange lines on the Martian surface. Schiaparelli's maps of Mars show crisscrossing lines that he called *canali*, an Italian word meaning 'channels' or 'canals'.

The most famous of early Mars observers was an American named 📍 Percival Lowell. He was fascinated by Mars, and by Schiaparelli's reports of its *canali*. By 1894, Lowell had built an observatory in Flagstaff, in Arizona, with a telescope that he used to study Mars. Over a number of years, Lowell reported seeing faint lines on Mars. He believed that these lines were canals created by human-like beings to transport water from polar ice caps to Martian deserts. Despite a great deal of evidence that showed Mars was too dry and too cold for life, Lowell's maps of Martian canals inspired many science fiction stories about life on Mars.

Even the best telescope images of Mars are fuzzy. This is because of the great distance between Earth and Mars, and because Earth's atmosphere is never still. Only the largest features on the surface of Mars are visible so it's hard to know how Schiaparelli and Lowell recorded such detail.

HOW DO YOU SAY IT?

Schiaparelli: **scap**-ah-**rel**-ee
canali: **can**-al-ee

Giovanni Schiaparelli's maps of Mars show lines that he called *canali*. These hand-drawn maps were based on brief periods of clear viewing during long hours spent at the telescope.

Like Schiaparelli before him, Percival Lowell relied on brief periods of clear viewing to draw his maps. Lowell believed the 184 canals that he saw were dug by intelligent Martians. Other astronomers used similar telescopes to study Mars but were unable to see Lowell's canals.

Sampling Martian soil for microbes

In July 1965, when *Mariner 4*, the first robot spacecraft, flew past Mars, it sent photographs of Mars back to Earth. These few grey and grainy pictures suggested that Mars was more like Earth's Moon than a planet with intelligent beings living on it. These photographs destroyed Lowell's romantic images of Martians and their canals forever.

However, this did not mean that microbes could not live in the harsh Martian environment. In 1975, two American spacecraft, called *Viking 1* and *Viking 2*, were launched to Mars. These were the first robot spacecraft specifically designed to look for life beyond Earth. They both carried miniature laboratories to test for microbes in the Martian soil. When they successfully landed on Mars in 1976, scientists held their breath waiting for the pictures and test results. Although the photographs were stunning, the soil test results seemed to show that there were no organisms living in the Martian soil.

MARS FACTS

Mars is the third planet from the Sun
Diameter: 6,794 kilometers (4,212 miles)
Length of year: 687 Earth days
Length of day: 24 hours 37 minutes (Earth time)
Atmosphere: **carbon dioxide**
Average surface temperature: -55°C (-67°F)
Warmest surface temperature: 27°C (80°F)
Coldest surface temperature: -133°C (-207°F)

The view of the Martian surface from *Viking 2* on Utopia Planitia (the 'Plains of Utopia' on Mars). Despite the tests for life in the Martian soil apparently failing, later *Viking 2* photographs showed frosts that gave Utopia Planitia an eerie, Earth-like appearance.

Robot spacecraft and the *Hubble Space Telescope* have given us much sharper pictures of Mars. They also show that Schiaparelli's *canali* and Lowell's canals are not really there. The reason why both men saw straight lines where none exist is still a mystery.

Fossilized Martian microbes

In August 1996, **NASA** scientists announced that a **meteorite** from Mars may contain evidence of life. The meteorite, known as ✦ **ALH84001**, was found in Antarctica in 1984. Scientists even suggested that the meteorite may contain minute fossilized Martian microbes. They also made it clear that this was not conclusive proof of life on Mars.

Further scientific studies now show that ALH84001 may not have contained evidence of Martian microbes at all. So the question of life on Mars is still without a definite answer. There has been no evidence to prove that extraterrestrial life exists—yet.

The announcement that a Martian meteorite may contain evidence of ancient microbes made headline news around the world.

ALH84001 was formed on Mars 4.5 billion years ago. It was blasted into space by a powerful collision. It drifted through space for 15 million years, then fell to Earth in Antarctica around 13,000 years ago.

When scientists used a microscope to look closely at ALH84001, they found tiny sausage-shaped objects that look like bacteria from Earth. However, they are much smaller than Earth bacteria, and scientists now doubt whether they are fossilized Martian microbes at all.

Looking for life elsewhere in the Solar System

Extraterrestrial life on Europa

For a long time the search for life in our Solar System focused on Mars. This all changed in 1979 when a robot spacecraft, called ✈ *Voyager 1*, flew past the planet Jupiter and took close-up photographs of its moons. The photographs of Europa, one of Jupiter's four large moons, showed that Europa is mainly made of rock. It has a smooth surface, smoother than any other object in the Solar System, almost no craters, and is crisscrossed with dark lines.

Voyager 1 and *2* revealed that Europa's smooth surface is completely covered with ice that looks like the sea ice at Earth's poles. This means there may be an ocean under Europa's icy crust. Because water is so important to life on Earth, astrobiologists now think that Europa is a good place to search for extraterrestrial life. This search began in 1995 when a robot spacecraft, called ✈ *Galileo*, swung into orbit around Jupiter. Part of *Galileo*'s mission is to study and take photographs of Europa.

EUROPA FACTS

Europa is a moon of Jupiter	
Diameter:	3,138 kilometers (1,950 miles)
Composition:	rock with an icy crust
Time to orbit Jupiter:	3.6 Earth days
Length of day:	3.6 Earth days
Atmosphere:	oxygen (incredibly thin)
Average surface temperature:	-145°C (-230°F)

This close-up picture of Europa was taken by *Galileo*. It shows iceberg-like blocks, which means there may be an ocean of liquid water under the ice. On Earth, there is a lake 4 kilometers (2.5 miles) below Antarctic ice that may contain life. Could the same be true on Europa?

Europa's surface looks like a cracked eggshell. The white crust of ice is crisscrossed with long cracks, which suggests there may be liquid water beneath this ice. This ocean may be below as much as 50 kilometers (30 miles) of ice.

The origin of life on Titan

After leaving Jupiter, *Voyager 1* continued its journey of exploration. Late in 1980, it flew past Saturn, with Saturn's large moon Titan in its sights. Astronomers already knew that Titan is the only moon with a thick atmosphere. They also thought Titan was the largest moon in the Solar System. They now know that Titan is actually smaller than Ganymede, another of Jupiter's moons.

Titan has a thick hazy atmosphere that is made mainly of nitrogen. Nitrogen is also the main gas in Earth's atmosphere. Titan's atmosphere also contains small amounts of **methane** and **organic chemicals**. This means that Titan's present atmosphere may be similar to Earth's atmosphere when life first formed on Earth. That was four billion years ago and Earth's atmosphere has changed a great deal since then. Titan's atmosphere, however, has not changed at all. Astrobiologists are studying Titan to try to learn more about the origin of life on Earth.

The *Hubble Space Telescope* was recently able to see through Titan's clouds and haze to reveal light regions. These light regions may be continents surrounded by an ocean of liquid ethane, an organic chemical. A weird world indeed!

Even in this *Voyager* photograph, Titan's surface is hidden by dense orange haze and clouds. It was this thick haze that first made it so difficult to know Titan's size. Scientists have suggested that ethane may rain out of the orange clouds onto Titan's surface.

TITAN FACTS

Titan is a moon of Saturn

Diameter: 5,150 kilometers (3,200 miles)

Composition: rock and ice

Time to orbit Saturn: 15.9 Earth days

Length of day: 15.9 Earth days

Atmosphere: nitrogen

Average surface temperature: -180°C (-290°F)

Signs of early life on asteroids and comets

The smaller members of the Solar System are called 🚀 asteroids and 🚀 comets. Asteroids are small, rocky objects. They are usually found orbiting the Sun between Mars and Jupiter, in a broad band called the main belt. Astrobiologists are interested in asteroids because they are the leftover bits from when the Solar System was formed. They hope asteroids will tell us about the Solar System at a time before there was life on Earth.

Comets are small objects made of ice and dust. Like asteroids, they are bits left over from the formation of the Solar System. Countless millions of comets orbit the Sun well beyond Pluto. Astrobiologists are interested in comets because they contain organic chemicals that could tell us about the first types of life on Earth.

HOW DO YOU SAY IT?

Dactyl: **dak**-til

Giotto: gee-**ot**-oh

🚀 Comet Halley as seen from Earth in 1986. It will return in 2061. A comet's tail is made up of gas and dust that are pushed away from its nucleus (the icy middle of its body) by solar wind. Halley's tail is millions of miles long, but is incredibly thin.

This is an asteroid known as ✈ Ida. Ida was photographed in 1993 by a robot spacecraft called *Galileo* as it flew through the main belt on its way to Jupiter. Ida is 52 kilometers (32 miles) long and is orbited by its own tiny moon, called ✈ Dactyl.

The robot spacecraft ✈ *Giotto* flew within 605 kilometers (376 miles) of Comet Halley's 16-kilometer-long (10 mile) nucleus. This photograph shows the dark-black nucleus giving off gas and dust. Some astrobiologists believe that the black material may be made of organic chemicals.

Space technology
On the way to Titan and a comet

The Space Age officially began on October 1, 1957. This was when Russia launched *Sputnik 1*, the world's first artificial satellite. Until then, telescopes were the only instruments that astronomers could use to study the Solar System. The launch of *Sputnik 1* signalled the development of rockets and spacecraft that allowed more direct exploration of the Solar System. Robot spacecraft are still used today to explore far distant planets, moons, asteroids and comets.

Since the early days of the Space Age, every planet (except Pluto, because it is so far away from Earth) in the Solar System has been visited at least once by robot spacecraft. Most simply fly past a planet and its moons, take photographs and gather information, and return these to Earth. These photographs and information have helped astrobiologists identify the best places to search for life beyond Earth.

Saturn's large moon Titan is one place where scientists are searching for organic chemicals associated with life. A spacecraft called *Cassini* is now on its way to orbit Saturn. *Cassini* will use radar to see through Titan's hazy atmosphere and map its surface. It will also release a small probe (another name for a type of robot spacecraft) called *Huygens*. *Huygens* will investigate Titan's atmosphere, and possibly even land on its surface.

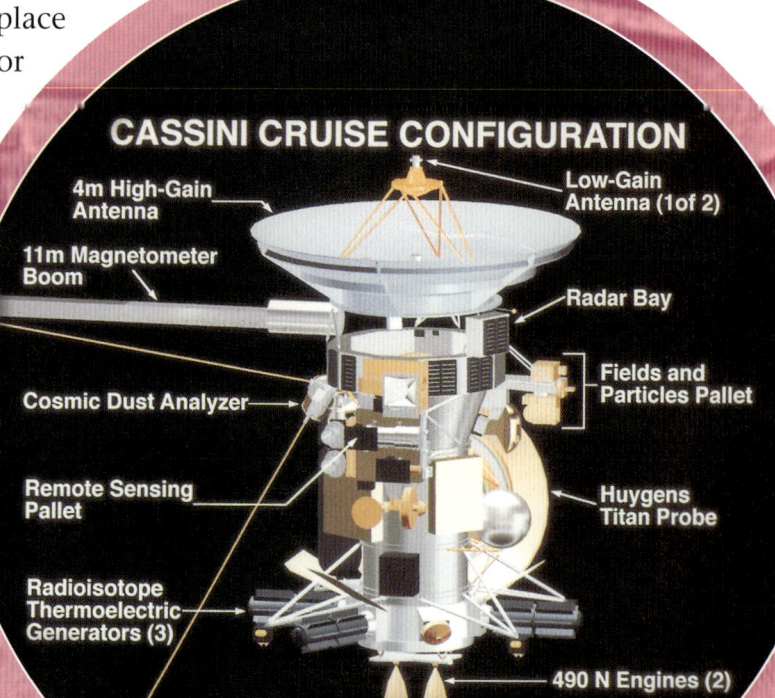

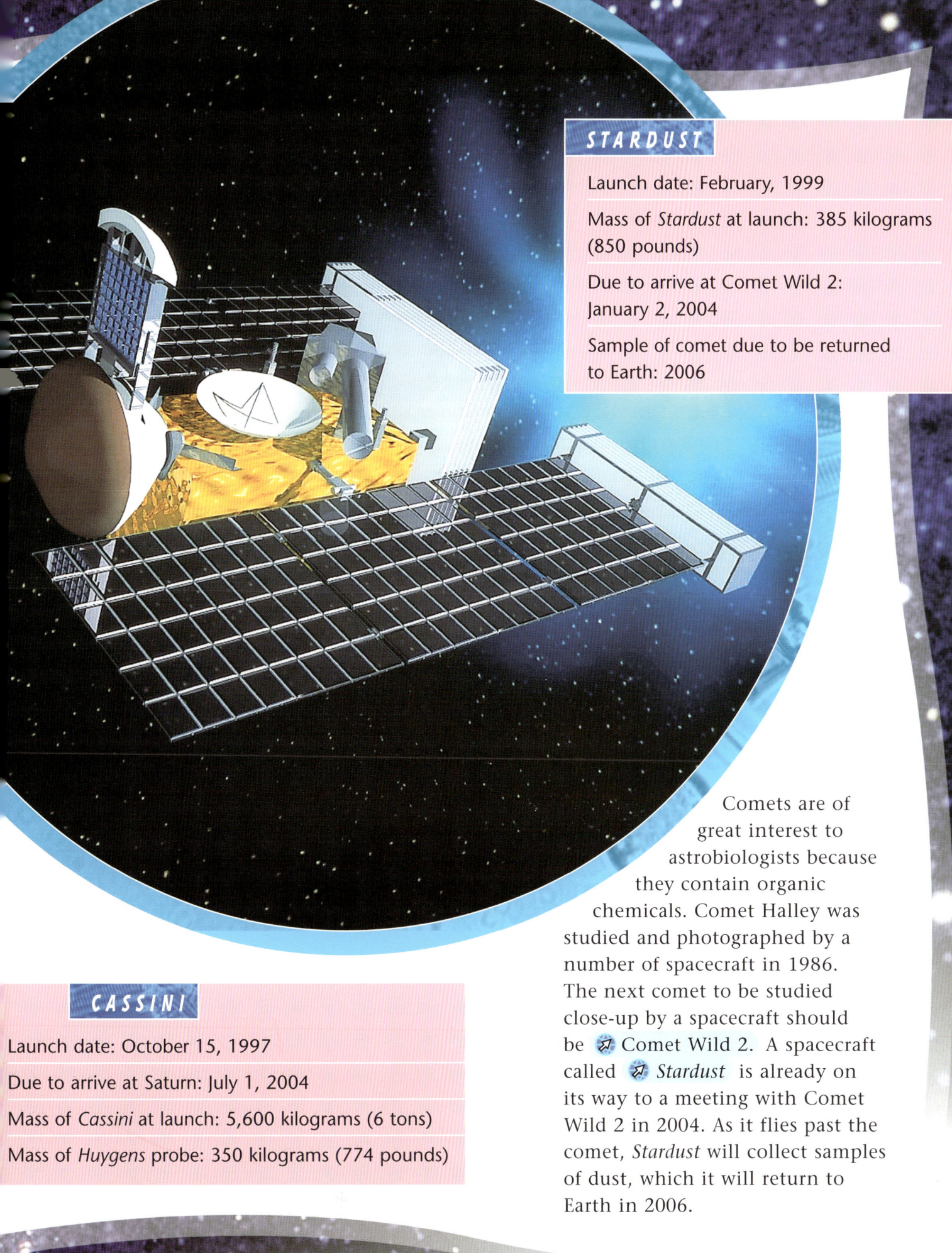

STARDUST

Launch date: February, 1999

Mass of *Stardust* at launch: 385 kilograms (850 pounds)

Due to arrive at Comet Wild 2: January 2, 2004

Sample of comet due to be returned to Earth: 2006

CASSINI

Launch date: October 15, 1997

Due to arrive at Saturn: July 1, 2004

Mass of *Cassini* at launch: 5,600 kilograms (6 tons)

Mass of *Huygens* probe: 350 kilograms (774 pounds)

Comets are of great interest to astrobiologists because they contain organic chemicals. Comet Halley was studied and photographed by a number of spacecraft in 1986. The next comet to be studied close-up by a spacecraft should be Comet Wild 2. A spacecraft called *Stardust* is already on its way to a meeting with Comet Wild 2 in 2004. As it flies past the comet, *Stardust* will collect samples of dust, which it will return to Earth in 2006.

Continuing the search for extraterrestrial life

The Solar System is an incredibly big place. The distances between planets are measured in millions, or even billions, of miles. Travel times are measured in years. These distances are too great for humans to travel, so robot spacecraft are used to explore the Solar System. Some spacecraft have simply flown past planets while others have been placed in orbit around planets. A few spacecraft have even landed on Venus and Mars.

Not all spacecraft have been successful. The difficulty of exploring the Solar System was highlighted in 1999 when two spacecraft, *Mars Climate Orbiter* and *Mars Polar Lander*, both failed. Nevertheless, robot spacecraft have recently been launched towards Saturn and the Comet Wild 2. Other planned cometary spacecraft include *Contour*, *Rosetta* and *Deep Impact*. Soon new spacecraft will be launched to continue searching for life on Mars and Europa.

In 2003 NASA plans to launch two robot spacecraft that will each land a rover (shown here) on the surface of Mars in 2004. The *Mars 2003* rovers could then be followed by robot spacecraft that will return Mars rocks to astrobiologists on Earth.

MARS SAMPLE RETURN

Original plans were for a launch in June, 2003. This would have returned Mars rocks to Earth in April, 2008. The failure of *Mars Polar Lander* has delayed these plans.

EUROPA ORBITER

Planned launch date: November, 2003

Planned arrival at Jupiter: 2006

Planned orbit of Europa: 2008

The possibility that there may be an ocean on Europa now fascinates astrobiologists. Photographs and information from *Voyager* and *Galileo* did not prove that this ocean exists, so NASA plans to send a new spacecraft to Europa. This new spacecraft, called *Europa Orbiter,* will be equipped with radar that should be able to see through Europa's icy crust. If this ocean does exist, future spacecraft may be sent to Europa to look for life.

Profile of an astronomer and exobiologist
Dr. Carl Sagan

In 1980, a program called 'Cosmos' was shown on television. 'Cosmos' was seen by 500 million people in 60 countries—more viewers than any other public series before it. 'Cosmos' was written and presented by Dr. Carl Sagan, an American astronomer and exobiologist. Although he was a scientist, Dr. Sagan is best known as a science communicator. Through his television programs and many books, Dr. Sagan taught many people about the scientific exploration of space and the search for extraterrestrial life.

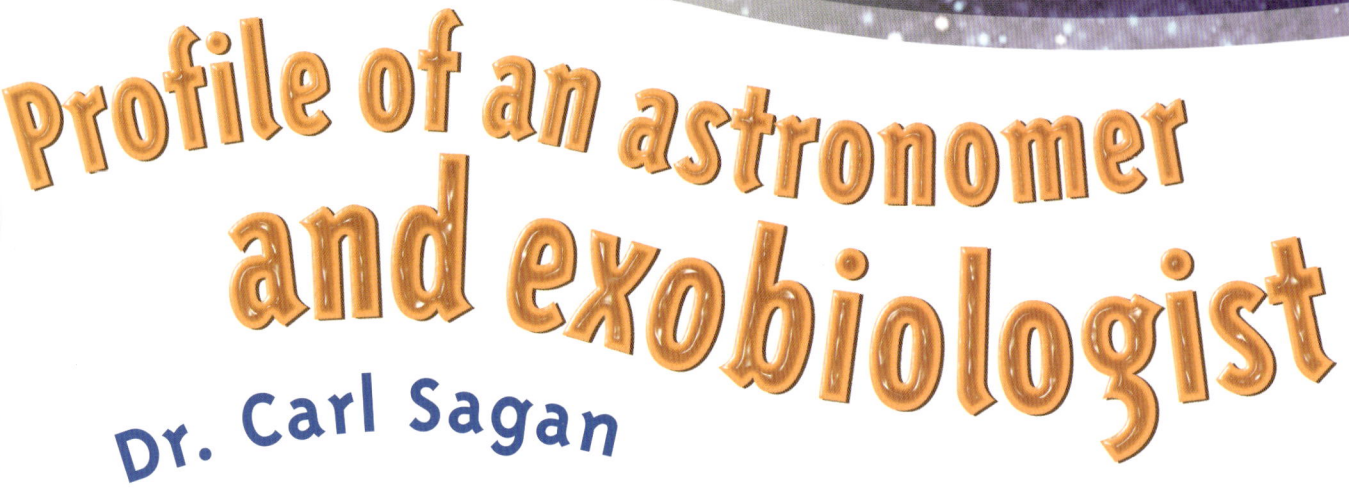

Carl Sagan was born in 1934, and from an early age he was interested in astronomy and the possibility of life beyond the Earth. As a scientist, Dr. Sagan worked as an adviser to NASA on the *Apollo* moon program. He was also a member of the scientific teams that used robot spacecraft (including *Mariner*, *Viking*, *Voyager* and *Galileo*) to explore the Solar System. As an astronomer and exobiologist, Dr. Sagan helped to study the Solar System, and promoted the search for extraterrestrial life. Dr. Carl Sagan died at the age of 62 on December 20, 1996.

On July 4, 1997, the *Pathfinder* spacecraft landed on Mars. Its landing site was named the Sagan Memorial Station in memory of Dr. Carl Sagan who died shortly after *Pathfinder's* launch. This is a fitting tribute to a man who devoted his life to astronomy and exobiology.

Four robot spacecraft are now travelling beyond our Solar System. Dr. Sagan convinced NASA to include messages, such as *Voyagers*' 'Sounds of Earth' recording (cover shown here). If *Voyager 1* or *Voyager 2* are eventually found by extraterrestrials, these recordings will show what life on Earth is like.

Exploring new frontiers

Looking beyond the Solar System

Astronomers know that there are billions of stars in our own galaxy, the Milky Way. They also know that the Milky Way is only one of billions of galaxies in the Universe. Until recently, though, they did not know if any of these other stars were surrounded by their own solar systems (planets, moons, asteroids and comets).

The Universe is so big that any planets orbiting other stars have, until recently, been too far away and too faint to see from Earth. Although they are still too far away to see, astronomers have been able to use other methods to find large planets as they orbit other stars. In 1995, a large planet was found orbiting a star called 51 Pegasi. Since that time, the same method has been used to find large planets orbiting a number of other stars. The next step for astronomers and astrobiologists is to get pictures of the planets in other solar systems.

The *Hubble Space Telescope* is the first large telescope in space. Although it provides a better view of the Universe than Earth-based telescopes, it cannot see other solar systems. Future space-based telescopes, such as *Kepler*, are in the planning stages. One day, they may find Earth-like planets orbiting other stars.

We can see countless stars from Earth, but we cannot yet see planets that may be orbiting these stars. If planets do orbit some of these stars, do they hold life?

Finding out more

Books like this one only give a brief introduction to a subject as broad as extraterrestrial life. Some other useful reference books are:

Bill Yenne, *The Atlas of the Solar System*, Bison Books, 1988
Carl Sagan, *Cosmos*, Abacus, 1985
Carl Sagan, *Pale Blue Dot: A Vision of the Human Future in Space*, Headline, 1995
David McNab and James Younger, *The Planets*, BBC Books, 1999
Paul Raeburn, *Mars: Uncovering the Secrets of the Red Planet*, National Geographic Society, 1998
Ronald Greeley and Raymond Batson, *The NASA Atlas of the Solar System*, Cambridge University Press, 1997

You may also find the following web sites useful:

www.nasa.gov
NASA is the American space agency. This is its web site.

www.jpl.nasa.gov
NASA's Jet Propulsion Laboratory.

www.iki.rssi.ru
This is the web site of the Russian space agency.

www.esrin.esa.it
This is the web site of the European space agency.

photojournal.jpl.nasa.gov
This web site includes NASA photographs of planets and moons.

www.anu.edu.au/Physics/nineplanets/nineplanets.html
The Nine Planets, a multimedia tour of the Solar System.

www.solarviews.com/eng/homepage.htm
Views of the Solar System.

astrobiology.arc.nasa.gov
NASA's astrobiology home page.

As urls (web site addresses) may change, you may have trouble finding a site listed here. If this happens, you can still use the key words highlighted throughout the book to search for information about a topic.

Glossary

bacteria: Simple, single-celled microscopic organisms

carbon dioxide: A gas that makes up a small part of Earth's atmosphere, but is the major component of the atmospheres of Venus and Mars

extreme environments: Places where it is hard for organisms to survive because it is very hot, very cold, or very dry

hydrothermal vents: Hot springs on the sea floor

meteorite: A piece of extraterrestrial rock or metal that has landed on the Earth. (A meteor is the fiery trail made by a meteorite as it passes through the Earth's atmosphere)

methane: An explosive gas that is made of hydrogen and carbon

moons: Objects that orbit a planet or another object, such as an asteroid

NASA: The National Aeronautics and Space Administration

orbiting: Travelling around

organic chemical: A substance that contains carbon, usually combined with oxygen, hydrogen and nitrogen. Many organic chemicals are made by living organisms

planets: Large objects that orbit stars. The Earth is a planet orbiting a star we call the Sun

robot spacecraft: Automatic vehicles that travel outside Earth's atmosphere without humans aboard

satellite: An object, either natural or artificial, that orbits a planet or another body

solar system: A collection of planets, moons, comets and asteroids that orbits a star. Our Solar System consists of the Sun (our star), nine planets (Mercury, Venus, Earth, Mars, Jupiter, Saturn, Uranus, Neptune and Pluto), numerous moons and countless comets and asteroids

solar wind: A constant stream of particles that moves out from the Sun in all directions

Index

51 Pegasi 28

A
asteroids 6, 20, 21

B
bacteria 8, 15

C
Cassini 22, 23
Comet Halley 20, 21, 23
Comet Wild 2 23, 24
comets 4, 6, 20, 23
Contour 24

D
Dactyl 21
Deep Impact 24

E
Earth-like planets 7, 29
Europa 5, 6, 9, 16, 17, 25
Europa Orbiter 25
extreme environments 4, 8

G
Galileo 16, 17, 21, 25, 26
Giotto 21

H
Hubble Space Telescope 13, 18, 29
Huygens 22

I
Ida 21

J
Jupiter 5, 9, 16, 18, 20, 25

K
Kepler 29

L
Lowell, Percival 10, 11

M
Mariner 4 12
Mars 5, 6, 8, 9, 10, 11, 12, 13, 20, 24
Mars 2003 24
Mars Climate Orbiter 24
Mars Polar Lander 24
Martian meteorite ALH84001 14, 15

P
Pathfinder 27
Pluto 6, 20

R
Rosetta 24

S
Sagan, Dr. Carl 26, 27
Sagan Memorial Station 27
Saturn 5, 18, 19, 22, 23, 24
Schiaparelli, Giovanni 10, 11
'Sounds of Earth' 27
Sputnik 1 22
Stardust 23

T
Titan 5, 6, 18, 19, 22

V
Venus 6, 24
Viking 1 12
Viking 2 12, 13
Voyager 1 16, 18, 27
Voyager 2 16, 27